This book belongs to:

molly o'donnell

4

BRILLIANT

A catalogue record for this book is available from the British Library

Published by Ladybird Books Ltd
80 Strand WC2R 0RL
A Penguin Company

2 4 6 8 10 9 7 5 3 1
© LADYBIRD BOOKS LTD MMVII
LADYBIRD and the device of a Ladybird are trademarks of Ladybird Books Ltd

ISBN-13: 9781846464980
ISBN-10: 1846464986

Printed in Italy

The Princess and the Pea

illustrated by
Marie-Anne Didier-Jean

pea

prince

queen

4

princess

mattress

bed

5

Once there was a prince. The prince wanted to marry. But he only wanted to marry a real princess.

"Is she a real
princess?" asked
the prince.
"No," said the queen.
"She is not a real
princess."

"Is she a real princess?" asked the prince.
"No," said the queen.
"She is not a real princess."

One day, a girl came
to see the prince.

"Is she a real
princess?" asked
the prince.
"We will see," said
the queen.

The queen put
a pea in the bed.
She put a mattress
on the pea.

The queen put
another mattress
on the bed.
Then she put on
another and another
and another.

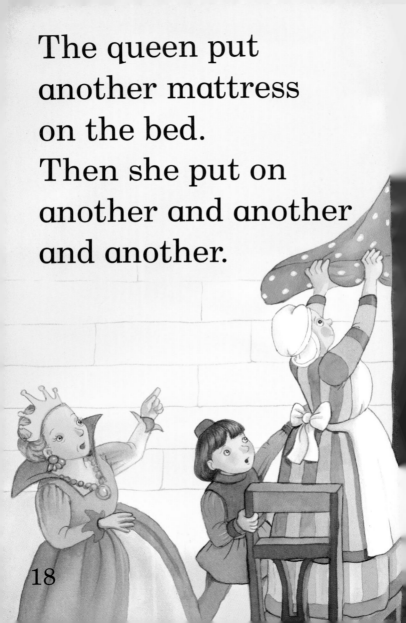

The girl went to bed.
The next day, the
queen asked the girl,
"Did you sleep well?"

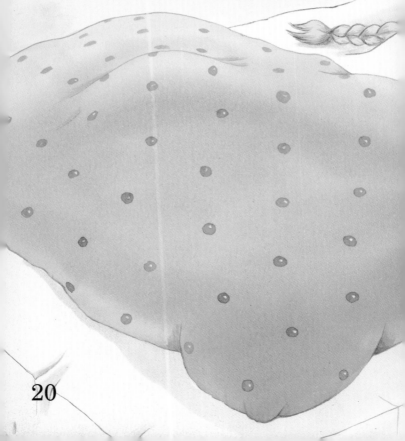

21

"No," said the girl,
"I did not sleep well.
There was something
in the bed."

22

"Is she a real
princess?" asked
the prince.
"Yes!" said the queen.
"She is a real
princess."

"Will you marry me?"
asked the prince.
"Yes!" said the girl.
"But only if you are
a real prince!"